Fartucus Pugsly

The Sad and Smelly Saga of a Pungent Pug

Emery Trax

Fartucus Pugsly
The Sad and Smelly Saga of a Pungent Pug

Copyright 2017 Emery Trax

Fartucus Pugsly is a work of fiction. Any resemblance to students, teachers, or dogs in your city is probably a coincidence. All characters, situations, and events are the original creation of the author.

Published in the United States

ISBN-13: 978-1542367219
ISBN-10: 1542367212

Table of Contents

The Purse Poodle Did It

I was framed! And I didn't do nothing!

Well, almost nothing…because you see, I was innocent, until I was proven guilty by a judge named B.B. Diggs. He's a cat lover, and doesn't like Pugs. So there you go!

It all began when I was walking myself down to the Squatter's Dog Park to hang out with my friends, Rocky and Bella.

Halfway there a pointy nosed woman wearing a blue bird's nest hat click-clacked out of the Madam Finecki's Pet Shop Boutique. She held a fancy alligator skin purse tucked beneath her left arm. A quivering and rather snotty nose poked out of the purse, sniffed the air, and sneezed.

"That's digusting," the woman said and crinkled her pointy nose. "You should be ashamed."

Only she wasn't talking to her prim and proper little Purse Poodle, with the pink ribbon in her hair and a snotty nose. She was talking to me.

"Chloe," the pointy nosed woman screeched and clasped a protective hand over Chloe's nose. "Don't breathe, girl. Mama will get you out of here."

"What'd I do?" I asked and looked to the Poodle for help.

Chloe winked and growled in my direction. "I did it," she said and ran her tiny red tongue over her snotty nose. "But I'm not telling."

Purse dogs, I thought and scowled. Who needs them?

And to be honest, I didn't give it another thought. I mean, when you're a Pug, you get used to being blamed for everything.

If Stevie's rubber duck gets its tail chewed off, the Pug did it. If Jessie's doll loses its head, the Pug did it. And if a cloud of stench suddenly envelopes the living room right during the exciting part of a *Gilligan's Island* rerun, the Pug did it.

I'm the Pug. Fartucus Pugsly is my name…and everybody's always picking on me.

But so what? When you're as wide-eyed handsome and well put together as me, you get used to being blamed for stuff. It happens. Life goes on.

Only this time, my brief encounter with the pointy nosed woman and a Purse Poodle named Chloe, set the stage for the end of my life as I knew it.

Everything, and I mean everything, was about to change.

And it wasn't even fair.

Mail Truck Mayhem

Comfortably numb and clueless to what lie ahead of me, I went about my day.

As usual, I stopped by Madam Finecki's Pet Shop Boutique to play peek-a-boo with the critters in the window display.

A fresh batch of Dalmatian pups in the pet shop window wrestled around and tried to look cute for all the kids walking to school.

Behind the basket of puppies, a gruesome looking and very squirmy Boa Constrictor gulped his breakfast and stared at me with these beady little eyes that said, "You're next."

Yikes!

"Gag me and drop me in the river," I said and skipped off the sidewalk and into the traffic. Who in their right mind wants a snake for a pet? I mean, think about it. They're not warm and cuddly like Pugs. They can't like your face or clean up the supper leftovers like a Pug. And they're certainly not as fun to have around as a Pug.

Fact is, the way I saw it, a Pug was the perfect all-around pet for any family.

Anyways, like I was saying, it was a beautiful day, and everything was perfect as apple pie a la mode…until a careening mail truck tried to ruin my day!

Rrrrr! Screeeech! Wham!

The mail truck leapt onto the sidewalk in a clear violation of Squatsylvania City Ordinance 13-1, proceeded south for approximately eight feet at great speed, and crashed to a violent stop halfway through the front door of the pet shop boutique.

Steam whistled into the air from the mail truck's ruptured radiator, and letters, bills, and jury notices rained from the sky like burnt chunks of confetti during a fireworks show where they accidentally set off all the Fire Ball Stars at once.

That was close, I thought and looked over my shoulder at the mayhem.

The pups were overjoyed at all the excitement and yapped like mad when the fire truck bell clanged in the distance.

The snake, doing what snakes do best, used the chaos and confusion to his advantage and squiggled his way out the broken window and between the feet of a confused police officer who couldn't help but blow his whistle and shout, "Nothing to see hear folks."

"Got mice?" the snake hissed and tasted the air with his forked tongue. "I'm hungry."

"Fresh out," I said and scratched a pesky flea off my ear. "But don't blame me if you get smashed by a mail truck, or something."

"Right-o," the snake hissed and slithered into a handy storm drain.

It was a grand show, and everybody was having fun…except the mailman.

"Dab blasted, bulgy-eyed, tongue lapping, smelly curly-tailed, smashed up face, four legged menace to man and beast," the mail man screamed and pointed at me.

"There he is. He did this."

See what I mean? A mail truck crashes through a pet shop window, and what do you do? You blame the Pug, of course. I didn't do it. I didn't do nothing.

All I wanted to do was get to Squatter's Dog Park for a play date with Rocky and Bella.

But like I said, when you're a wide-eyed handsome devil like myself, doing something calm and ordinary, like hanging out in the park, is next to impossible.

Here I Come to Save the Day...NOT

It's a strange truth about life...you never really know what you're good at until you are challenged.

In my case, I never knew I was a superhero, until I walked across the street towards the green grocer's store and came face to face with a sloppy faced Rottweiler lifting his leg on a mound of bananas.

I mean, this guy was all rippling muscles and razor sharp teeth.

Two shoestring threads of drool hung from his thick jowls, and he had this look about him that said, "Feed me, or else."

"Whoa, buddy," I said and raced forward to stop the violation. "This ain't no fire hydrant."

"Yeah, well this ain't no peep show, either," the Rottweiler growled back. "Mind your own business."

The Rottweiler shook his head, splattering the bananas with oozing wads of dog spit, and then strutted off like he was the reincarnation of Kaiser Wilhelm, or something.

"That's just too much," a man in a red and white checked apron moaned. "My bananas…they're soiled."

And then he looked at me.

"You did this!"

I shook my head and licked my lips. Get real guy, I thought. Do I look like a dog that can pee on a stack of bananas on a table? I mean, even with a ladder I would have a hard time pulling that off…super hero or not.

But, you can't talk sense to a maniac. As far as the green grocer man was concerned, the only sensible thing to do at the time was to blame it on the Pug.

"This is the fifth time this week," the grocer said and grabbed his broom. "This time I caught you red-handed. You're going down…as in downtown!"

Whack!

The stiff bristles of the broom crashed into the bananas like a Babe Ruth home run swing of the bat. Bananas rolled off the table, across the sidewalk, and into the street.

It was a royal mess…and it was not my fault.

"Bananas, they're everywhere," the grocer cried and swung the broom again.

"Get out of here, you…you…menace to society."

"Well, you don't have to tell me twice," I grumbled and tucked my tail as I kicked the old pistons into over drive…only to run headlong into a lady carrying a bouquet of fresh cut daisies.

And it's a good thing I like daisies, because I got a mouthful!

"My bananas," I heard the grocer groan as I rounded the corner.

"My daisies," the flower lady cried.

"You're going to jail," the Rottweiler said from a hiding spot in the alley. "Yes sir, all the way to the clinker for you."

"But, I didn't do nothing," I protested.

"Doesn't matter. You're a Pug. The Pug always gets the blame when bad things happen."

And then he yelped and jumped a mile into the air.

"Snake!"

My Boa Constrictor friend shook his head at the whimpering Rottweiler and tasted the air with his tongue.

"What gives in this town, anyway? I can't find a mouse anywhere. I'm going back to the pet shop."

No Steamy Piles Allowed, Thank You

Okay, by now I was late. Rocky and Bella agreed to meet me first thing in the morning, after breakfast…and I was late already!

I cut through a dark alley, dodged a pack of rats living out of a dumpster behind my favorite pizza place, and strolled onto Squatter's Lane.

"Get back," a lady in high heeled shoes and a fancy dress yelled and pulled her Yorkie close to her with one of those leashes that wind up when you press a button.

The Yorkie yelped, gasped for breath, and then turned his anger at me.

"Look what you made her do, you…you…ugly, smelly pugnacious Pug dog."

Well, now I had heard everything. It wasn't my fault he was born a Yorkie. And it was not my fault he chose to be walking down the street at the same time as me.

As for the smelly part…well, that was not my fault either. I was born with a bad digestive system. Besides, this was my street. I lived here.

"Going to the park?" I asked and rubbed against the little tyke.

"What's it to you?" the Yorkie replied and scratched his ear.

"Cut the act, boy," I said and watered a handy fire hydrant. "You don't have fleas."

Suddenly, like, without warning, the Yorkie plopped onto his butt and began to viciously scratch his ear.

"Oh, my goodness, a flea," the lady in high heels and a fancy pants dress screamed and pulled the poor guy into her protective arms. "You dirty Pug. You gave my Bandit fleas."

"Bandit?" I said and nearly tripped over a half-eaten hot dog some thoughtful kid had dropped.

I snarfed up the hot dog, gulped it down with half a chew, and turned my attention back to Bandit.

"Are you a pirate? Do you rob banks? Or did you get that name from stealing from the cat's litter box?"

Bandit turned his nose up at me and growled. "I do not eat cat litter."

"Hey, it's nothing to me. When a guy's gotta eat, a guy's gotta eat," I said and trotted ahead of the fancy pants dynamic duo. "See you at the park, Bandit."

****

It was a glorious day to be a dog. The sun was out, it was halfway warm, and kids were everywhere, dropping their triple scoop chocolate ice creams, munching on roasted garlic crackers, and best of all, tossing their cookies.

"Yo, Fartucus," Bella barked from across the park. "Over here."

"On my way," I shouted. "Just need to take care of some quick business, first."

Now, if you've ever been to a dog park, you know there are strict rules about cleaning up after yourself. It's called a *Leave No Trace* policy, and means your human friends have to pick up what you drop.

Well, you've probably figured out by now that I'm on my own. I'm my own man, you could say. So, when I dropped my load next to the picnic table in the kiddie section, I left a trace of my passing…a big, steamy, smelly trace.

I scratched the grass for three seconds in a foolish attempt to cover it up, and then bounced away, feeling a hundred pounds lighter, and ready for action.

Half a second later I heard this ear piercing scream.

"My genuine Italian designer label leather high heels. Ruined."

Sure enough, it was the fancy pants dress lady with her high heels, and her little Yorkie, too.

Bandit whimpered, and then glared in my direction.

"He did it," a little girl in pigtails with a triple scoop chocolate mint ice cream cone said. "The little Pugsly dog."

Busted.

Twenty sets of eyes turned on me.

"Not nice," a German Shepherd Police dog said.

"Yeah, who put you in charge?" I replied and flicked my curly tail at him.

I didn't see what all the fuss was about. I mean, so a lady got a little poo on her shoe. You're in a dog park. What do you expect?

"Somebody call the Dog Catcher," the lady in high heels said. "That Pug belongs in jail."

"They'll have to catch me first," I yapped back to the over grown police dog as I threw my hind legs into high gear and scooted out of there.

Peek a Boo, I Smell You

Just my luck.

All I ever wanted to do was goof around in the park with my friends, snag a few ice creams from the kids, and maybe dig up an old bone, or something.

But *NO*. The entire world wanted to ruin my day. And now the long arm of the law was after me!

"He went that way," the lady in the soiled high heels and fancy pants dress said and pointed towards the pond where I had run.

I hid in a stand of cattails next to the pond and watched as the Dog Catcher swatted the cattails with his butterfly net.

"Here, puppy. Come to papa," the Dog Catcher said and snarled. "Come to papa, you smelly little miscreant."

Get a life, I thought and crawled into a thicker stand of weeds and grass next to the water.

"Come out, we have you surrounded," the Dog Catcher lied.

And in a perfect example of horrible timing, I felt my stomach rumble. Sure enough, that half chewed hot dog I ate earlier was coming back to haunt me.

Phfft!

A cloud of dog fumes erupted out of the grass and drifted in the breeze towards the Dog Catcher.

The Dog Catcher dropped his net and cupped his hand over his nose.

"I smell you," he gagged and walked right to me.

What could I do? I was trapped, and I am not one of those water dogs you see in reality T.V. shows, so swimming for it was not an option. In fact, I've never even had a bath.

"Gotcha," the Dog Catcher yelled and swooped his butterfly net over me.

It looked like it was going to be curtains for poor Fartucus Pugsly…and it didn't help when every dog and human in the park, except maybe Rocky and Bella, cheered when they hauled me away.

It was like the worst perp walk in the history of forever.

Throw Away the Key

In a clear miscarriage of justice, a guy with white donut frosting on his lips and a gold badge on his belt led me into the courtroom to a round of boos and hisses.

"Put a cork in it," the pointy nosed lady with the Purse Poodle shouted from the gallery.

"Throw away the key," the mail man screeched as he struggled to sort a mountain of mixed up letters, bills, and jury duty notices.

Wow, I thought. They must be doing a murder trial or something. Whoever the court was after, I felt sorry for him. People were mad, and I have to admit, in all the excitement my natural instincts got the best of me.

"Aggh," the judge gagged. "What's that smell?"

I smiled and did a little happy dance around the court as Rocky and Bella watched from the peanut gallery.

"You're the man, Fartucus," Rocky barked.

"Strut it, Pug," Bella howled.

It felt good to see so many familiar faces in the court. It was like a family reunion and a homecoming parade all at once.

"He soiled my banana display," the green grocer shouted and held up a dripping banana as evidence.

"He ate my daisies," the flower shop woman screamed and tossed a flowerless stem my way.

"He ruined my genuine Italian designer label leather shoes," the lady in the fancy pants dress said. "And, he gave my little Bandit fleas."

"Order. Order in the court," Judge B.B. Diggs shouted and rapped his gavel with a loud clack.

"He violated my leash law and broke my new net," the Dog Catcher roared and held up a ripped butterfly net.

The donut cop guy led me to the front of the courtroom. I looked up and gulped. Cat hair covered the judge's robe, and from the looks of things, he did not like Pugs.

Judge Diggs shuffled a stack of papers, adjusted his glasses, and stared down at me over his mile long nose.

"Fartucus Pugsly, you are hereby accused of violating the City of Squatsylvania Clean Air Act, aiding and abetting an escaped snake, endangering the life of six Dalmatian pups, interfering with the U.S. mail delivery, and half a dozen episodes of excessive flatulence and gross misbehavior."

Judge Diggs coughed, took a sip of water, and stared down at me. "Young man, how do you plead?"

I could only whimper, lick my lips, and beg the court for mercy.

"Sounds like a guilty plea to me," the judge said and rapped his gavel. "Bailiff, get him out of here and throw away the key. My Snickerdoodles is late for her declawing appointment."

****

So, there you have it.

I had my day in court, and lost. Big surprise, right? After all, whenever anything goes wrong, it's easy to blame the Pug.

All I wanted was to spend the day with a couple friends in the park…and the sweet smelling, puffed up and well-dressed Fart Squad do-gooders prevailed!

I was angry, frightened, and a bit saddened. It was all too much. My stomach grumbled and I felt that familiar cramp deep inside. Something deep, dark, and malodorous wanted out.

My tail bobbed and jerked, and for half a second my back legs went numb. And then it happened…a hair curling, brain cell frying, toxic cloud of green vapor descended upon the courtroom.

A woman in the front row twitched her nose, twisted her mouth into a zombie like howl as she jammed a dirty handkerchief over her face…and passed out.

"Gas. We're under attack," the Bailiff shouted and bolted for the backdoor. "Run for your lives."

"Protect the women and children," a noble and brave man in a derby hat with a white feather shouted as he skipped out a side door, coughing and wheezing.

"Every man for himself," commanded the Judge like he was suddenly appointed Captain of the Titanic.

"The Pug did it!" A woman pushing a baby pram screeched as she tried heroically to fan the air around her baby's face with a newspaper.

Right, I thought and smiled like only a deranged and very content Pug can smile.

I did it. It was my greatest creation.

Father would have been proud.

Fast Times in the Clinker

Life in the clinker is not so bad, I thought and dropped a steaming curly pile on the floor next to the door of my cell.

"Yo, clean up on aisle four," I barked to the donut eating Dog Catcher. "Get a move on, buster. I'm trying to pace back and forth here."

Which is about all you can in jail.

You pace. You eat. You make a mess. And then you go to sleep.

I missed my walks around town, something fierce. I missed playing tag with Rocky and Bella down at the park. And I missed cracking jokes about Purse Poodles and pampered Yorkies.

But, nobody ever said life was fair. Besides, I was making new friends.

Bart the one-eyed sheepdog lived in the cell next to me. He spent most of his days sleeping and dreaming about sheep, and never bothered nobody. Across from him was Sophie, a fine looking little Chihuahua who kept everybody awake at night with her constant yapping. I loved the little girl, but she had a thing or two to learn about pack living.

Anyways, I was looking at a long stretch of life in the pen, with no hope of ever being bailed out, when something weird happened, and changed everything.

****

"I said I'm looking for the perfect pet," a man in cowboy boots and blue jeans mumbled to the Dog Catcher. "I don't want no Purse Poodle or Yorkie dog. I want the best dog you got."

Double negatives and bad grammar and all, this was a guy worth taking home. I knew it right off, just from the sound of his voice. This was a man who could recognize quality dog material when he saw it.

I spun around in a circle, rubbed my bum on the concrete floor to make sure it was clean, and stuck out my tongue in the classic Pug pose—known far and wide for its ultimate cuteness.

"What's this guy's story?" the man in the boots said and jerked his thumb in my direction.

"Oh, no," the Dog Catcher said. "That's the infamous Fartucus Pugsly. He won't do. Serving a life sentence for multiple counts of gross behavior, he is."

My blood boiled. Just when things were finally looking up around here, that donut smacking bozo Dog Catcher was trying to mess it up.

My stomach rumbled, and I felt that old familiar twitch deep down inside my rumbly tummy.

Pfft!

Sweet. Silent but deadly. A green cloud of oozing poison slipped its creeping tendrils between the cell bars and gently worked their way upward, to the unsuspecting, ill-prepared nostrils, of the white frosting, donut smacking, Dog Catcher.

"Eww! Gads, man alive, I'm dying," the Dog Catcher howled and ran for the closest exit.

The man in the boots grimaced, covered his mouth with both hands, and turned to stare down at me.

"You did that?" he asked, and smiled.

I licked my lips, spun in a circle, and howled. "I'll be in town all week," I yapped. "Drop by any day for a free show. Or take me home for a bonus performance."

Home, Home on the Range

"You're just the pet I need," he said and laughed. "You're going to help me get rid of my relative problem."

"What's a relative," I mumbled to myself and pranced out of prison with my curly tail high. I was free. Free at last.

"All you gotta do is act naturally," the man in the boots said as we drove out of town.

An hour later we pulled into a windy driveway leading up to a beautiful ranch house.

"Ten thousand acres of prime rangeland," the man said and sighed. "Almost heaven, except…"

"Melvis, I need grocery money," a woman in curlers and one of those moo-moo tent things some women wear.

"And I need a new set of golf clubs," a man in a tweed jacket and funny looking little French Captain hat shouted from the porch.

"Meet the relatives," the man I came to know as Melvis said and scratched my left ear.

"They dropped in for the holidays about a year ago. Now they won't leave."

I had no idea how I was supposed to help Melvis with his relative problem. But I was game for anything. Besides, there were chickens nearby. I could smell them. Sweet, sassy, chickens.

"Meet Pugsly," Melvis said and let me out of the truck.

I'm the kind of guy who makes friends fast, so I didn't waste a second.

"Get back. I don't like dogs," the woman cried and swatted at me with a broom.

"He will eat my new golf clubs, sure enough," the man in the French hat and tweed pants moaned. "I won't have it."

"Nonsense. He's just a dog. Somebody to keep me company when I'm working the cows," Melvis said. "Make yourself at home in the kitchen, Pugsly. This is your home now."

And so my life of leisure began.

I was finally where I belonged, and it only took a couple minutes for me to work up a double-barreled blast that sent the woman howling form the kitchen.

"I can't live with this smelly Pug."

From there I took myself upstairs, where as luck would have it I found the man in the tweed pants and French hat rubbing some kind of sweet smelling oil on his leather golf bag.

"Stay away from my golf clubs," the man in the tweed pants and French hat shouted. "And don't even think about touching my Genuine Spanish Main Hand Sewn Leather golf bag.

"But it smells so good," I thought and twitched my nose.

"Get back. Go away. Go outside and play."

Now, there's something you need to know about Pugs. We don't like being told what to do. In fact, it gets on our nerves.

I growled at the man in the tweed pants and French hat, and just for good measure, sunk my teeth into his Genuine Spanish Main Hand Sewn Leather golf bag.

"My golf bag," the man cried.

"My stomach," I howled back and let it rip.

"I can't take it, the man in the tweed pants and French hat moaned as he bolted down the stairs. "Honey, pack your bags. We're leaving."

Three minutes later the relative problem was finished.

"You won't have us to kick around anymore, the woman shouted as their little green and white car backfired and raced down the long driveway and away.

Melvis reached down and scratched my left ear. "I owe you one, my friend."

And that's how Rocky, Bella, Sophie, and even old Bart came to live the good life with me and Melvis, at home on the range.

"Just one thing, Pugsly," Melvis said late one night as we all relaxed on the porch watching the sun set. "The next time you feel the urge, do us all a favor and take it out back, away from the house."

No problem, I thought, and squeezed off a final, silent but deadly, volley.

Made in the USA
Lexington, KY
11 May 2017